W9-AUZ-185

First published in the United States in 1989 by Picture Book Studio.
Reissued in the United States, Great Britain, Canada, Australia, and New Zealand in 2006
by North-South Books, an imprint of NordSüd Verlag AG, Gossau Zürich, Switzerland.

First published in Switzerland under the title *12 Fabeln von Aesop* .

Distributed in the United States by North-South Books Inc., New York.
Library of Congress Cataloging-in-Publication Data is available.
A CIP catalogue record for this book is available from The British Library.

ISBN-13: 978-0-7358-2068-5 (trade edition)
ISBN-10: 0-7358-2068-6 (trade edition)
10 9 8 7 6 5 4 3 2 1

ISBN-13: 978-0-7358-2069-2 (paperback edition)
ISBN-10: 0-7358-2069-4 (paperback edition)
10 9 8 7 6 5 4 3 2 1

AESOP'S FABLES

SELECTED AND ILLUSTRATED BY

LISBETH ZWERGER

NORTH-SOUTH BOOKS · NEW YORK · LONDON

TOWN MOUSE AND COUNTRY MOUSE

A Town Mouse went to visit his cousin in the country. This Country Mouse lived simply, and he was not rich, but he brought out all that he had to feed and entertain his honored guest. Dried beans and barley, acorns and a wild berry or two made up the meal he offered his guest. The Town Mouse picked and poked at his food, and finally said, "How can you stand to eat such stuff, and how can you live here surrounded by nothing but dirt and stubble? If this is the best you can do here in the country, then you must come away with me to the town, and let me show how a mouse should really live!" They set off at once, and late that night came to a large house. "Right this way," said the Town Mouse proudly, and marched into a dining room where there had been a dinner party earlier in the evening. Climbing up onto the table, the Country Mouse sat on the edge of a plate as though it were a throne, and watched his friend scurry about collecting an assortment of cake morsels, rich bits of cheese, buttered bread, and leftover wine. As they prepared to eat this feast, there was a sudden commotion, and two huge barking dogs bounded into the room, and practically leapt onto the table. The two mice fled for their lives, and hid in a narrow crack in the floor. When the coast was clear, the trembling Country Mouse said farewell to the Town Mouse. "Your house is grand, and the food is very fine, but I am going back to my dried seeds and my home in the fields."

Simple meals in safety taste better than feasts in fear.

THE MILKMAID AND HER PAIL

The milkmaid was going to market with her pail of milk balanced on her head. And as she walked along, she began to plan ahead: "I'll be well paid for this good rich milk, so I shall buy a dozen eggs. Twelve eggs will hatch out into a fine flock of poultry, so I'll sell some of my plump chickens for a good price, and buy myself the prettiest new dress anyone has ever seen. Whenever I go to market, all the fine young men will come and want a word with me, and won't the other girls be jealous then! But I won't care a bit, and I'll toss my head like this." And as she spoke she tossed her head back, and down went the pail like a stone. The milk was all spilled, and all of the milkmaid's lovely dreams were just a puddle by the path.

Don't count your chickens before they're hatched.

THE MAN AND THE SATYR

A Man and a Satyr became friends, and decided to live together. All went well until one day in the winter when the Satyr saw the Man blowing on his hands. "Why do you do that?" asked the Satyr. "To warm my hands," said the Man. A while later, when they sat down to eat a supper of steaming hot porridge, the Man raised his bowl to his mouth and blew on it. "And what do you do that for?" said the Satyr. "To cool my porridge," replied the Man. The Satyr got up from the table. "I'm leaving," he said.

"I cannot be friends with a man who blows hot and cold with the same breath."

THE SHEPHERD'S BOY AND THE WOLF

A Shepherd's Boy was tending his flock near a village, but found the task boring and lonely. He thought he would cause some excitement by pretending that a Wolf was attacking his sheep, so he shouted, "Wolf! Wolf!" The villagers came running with pitchforks and shovels to help him, but when they arrived there was no Wolf. This seemed like good fun to the Boy, so he tried his game again a few days later. The people came to his aid once more, but as before, they found nothing. Then one day a real Wolf *did* come out of the forest, and the Boy shouted as loud as he could, "Wolf! Wolf!" But the villagers thought the Boy was up to his tricks again, and ignored him. And so the Wolf enjoyed a hearty meal.

You cannot believe a liar even when he tells the truth.

THE HARES AND THE FROGS

The Hares had so many enemies and lived such worried, frantic lives that they did not know what to do. One day they all gathered together and resolved that rather than live in such fear, they would drown themselves in a nearby pond. But as they neared the bank of the pond, a troop of Frogs, so frightened by the noise of their approach, leaped with great alarm and confusion into the water and hid. One of the older Hares, who was wiser than the others, cried out to his companions, "Stop, my friends. Things are not as bad as they seem, for these creatures are even more timid than Hares."

There is always someone worse off than yourself.

THE MONKEY AND THE CAMEL

At a meeting of all the beasts, the Monkey stood up to dance and the group found his antics very entertaining. The great applause when he was finished aroused the envy of the Camel, who also wanted to be popular. So the Camel got up and began to dance and cavort like the Monkey, but he looked so ridiculous that all the animals laughed at him and drove him away.

Seeking popularity is the fastest way to lose friends.

THE FOX AND THE GRAPES

A hungry Fox wandered into a vineyard and spied a juicy-looking bunch of Grapes hanging on a trellis just above his head. "This is the thing for me," he said, and jumped up to pull the Grapes down, but they were just out of his reach. He stepped back to take a running start, and had no better luck than his first attempt. Again and again he jumped up after the Grapes. At last he gave up trying, and walked out of the vineyard with his nose in the air, saying, "I thought those Grapes were ripe, but now I see that they are sour."

It is easy to scorn what you cannot get.

THE HARE AND THE TORTOISE

A Hare was always boasting about his speed and making fun of a Tortoise because he was so slow. One day the Tortoise challenged the Hare to a race. "You may laugh at me," he said, "but I know that I could beat you if we ran a race." The Hare was greatly amused at the idea of racing with a Tortoise, and so accepted the challenge. A course was set, and although the two started off together, the Hare quickly outran the Tortoise. He was so far ahead, in fact, that he decided to just lie right down and take a little nap. But the Hare overslept, and when he dashed to the finish line, there was the Tortoise. He had been plodding steadily forward all along, and had already won.

Slow and steady wins the race.

THE FOX AND THE CROW

A Crow was sitting on a branch of a tree with a piece of cheese in her beak when a Fox saw her and set about thinking of a way to get the cheese for himself. He went and stood under the tree, looked up and said to her, "How beautiful you look today! Your feathers are so glossy and your eye so bright. I am sure that if only you had a voice it would be more lovely than any other bird's." The Crow was much pleased by such praise, and wanted to prove that she could sing. She gave a loud "Caw!" but as soon as she opened her beak the cheese fell to the ground and the Fox snapped it up. "You can sing, I see," remarked the Fox, "but what you lack is brains."

Don't be fooled by flatterers.

THE DOG AND THE SOW

A Dog and a Sow were arguing. Each claimed that her own babies were better than those of the other. "Well," said the Sow at last, "at least mine can see when they are born, but yours are born blind." At that, the Dog huffed away, and never spoke to the Sow again.

Foolish comparisons lead to broken friendships.

THE MOON AND HER MOTHER

The Moon once asked her Mother to make her a gown. "How can I?" she replied. "There's no fitting you. At one time you're a New Moon, and at another you're a Full Moon, and in between you're neither one nor the other."

Nothing ever suits one who is always changing.

THE ASS AND THE LAP DOG

A Farmer one day came to the stables to see his beasts of burden. Among them was an Ass who was fed well with plenty of oats and hay, and who often carried his master. With the Farmer came his little Lap Dog, a great favorite, who danced and frisked about as happy and carefree as could be. The Farmer sat down to give some instructions to his stable hands, and the Lap Dog jumped in his lap and lay there blinking while the Farmer stroked his ears. Now the Ass became very jealous, for the Lap Dog led a life of leisure while his own life was full of labor, so he broke free from his halter and began to prance about just as he had seen the Lap Dog do. The Farmer held his sides with laughter, so the Ass went up to him and tried to climb into his lap, just as he had seen the Lap Dog do. At that the stable hands saw the danger that the Farmer was in, so they rushed up with sticks and pitch-forks and drove the Ass back to his stall. "Alas," cried the Ass.

"I was once respected for my honest labors, but by foolish jesting I have made an ass of myself."